Rotolo Middl

D0866705

DATE DUE

Meet the Kreeps

Three's a Krowd

by Kiki Thorpe

ROTOLO MIDDLE SCHOOL

T 61159   FIC THO

Three's a krowd

Scholastic Inc.
New York • Toronto • London • Auckland • Sydney
Mexico City • New Delhi • Hong Kong • Buenos Aires

If you purchased this book without a cover,
you should be aware that this book is stolen property.
It was reported as "unsold and destroyed" to the publisher,
and neither the author nor the publisher has received
any payment for this "stripped book."

No part of this publication may be reproduced, stored in
a retrieval system, or transmitted in any form or by any
means, electronic, mechanical, photocopying, recording,
or otherwise, without written permission of the publisher.
For information regarding permission, write to
Scholastic Inc., Attention: Permissions Department,
557 Broadway, New York, NY 10012.

ISBN-13: 978-0-545-13170-4
ISBN-10: 0-545-13170-7

Copyright © 2009 by Kiki Thorpe.
All rights reserved. Published by Scholastic Inc.
SCHOLASTIC, APPLE PAPERBACKS, and associated
logos are trademarks and/or registered trademarks of
Scholastic Inc.

12 11 10 9 8 7 6 5 4 3 2 1   9 10 11 12 13 14/0

Printed in the U.S.A.
First printing, July 2009

For my brother, Nick

❊ Chapter 1 ❊

Polly Winkler hurried outside to the Endsville Elementary School playground. She'd already missed fifteen minutes of recess. She didn't want to waste any more time.

Drat that Damon Kreep, she thought. Somehow, her weird stepbrother had gotten her into trouble again.

That afternoon, Polly's teacher, Mr. Crane, had thought *she* was responsible for the pencil shavings flying around the classroom, when Polly had only been trying to stop her stepbrother from setting off his

1

newest "scientific" invention. Damon called it a projectile agitator. Polly called it an exploding pencil sharpener. Either way, it had been Polly — not Damon — who'd had to stay indoors, cleaning, for the first half of recess.

Polly liked Mr. Crane, but when it came to Damon, the teacher didn't have a clue. Polly's stepbrother was a ten-year-old mad scientist, with a mind full of sinister schemes. But Mr. Crane thought he was just a smart, creative kid.

It was the same with the rest of Polly's stepfamily. There were Damon's pale, gloomy older brother, Vincent; their impish little sister, Esme; and their witch-like mother, Veronica. Each was odd in his or her own way, but put together they were the spookiest bunch Polly had ever met. They were more than just weird. Polly suspected they might have supernatural powers.

Strangely, no one else seemed to notice. Not Polly's sister, Joy, or her brother, Petey. Not even Polly's dad. They all thought Polly just had a big imagination.

All Polly wanted was a normal life. But it was tough to be normal with the Kreeps around. *Especially when Damon makes things like exploding pencil sharpeners*, Polly thought grimly.

She shook her long sand-colored bangs out of her eyes and looked around for her best friend, Mike. Finally, she spotted him out on the grass. He was kicking a soccer ball around with some other kids.

Polly started toward him. But just then the ball came to Mike, and he turned away, running toward the goal.

Polly sighed. It was too late for her to join

in the game. Now what was she supposed to do for the rest of recess?

Noticing that the monkey bars were free, Polly headed toward them. Usually, snotty Denise Dunleavy and her follow-along friends took over the monkey bars at recess. They liked to sit up there gossiping and looking down on the rest of the playground.

Polly went over to the bars and pulled herself up. She hooked her knees over a bar so she was hanging upside down. Then she began to swing her body back and forth, getting ready for a cherry drop.

Polly was midswing when someone walked up and stopped right in front of her. From where she was hanging, all Polly could see were two spotless white sneakers. Her gaze traveled up a pair of blue jeans and over a pink T-shirt, and came to rest on the upside-down face of Denise Dunleavy.

"Look," Denise said loudly. "There's a monkey on the monkey bars."

Denise's friend Misty snickered.

"Get off, Polly," Denise said. "These are *our* bars."

Polly gritted her teeth. Denise thought she was better than everyone just because her parents bought her nice clothes and took her on fancy vacations. Usually, when Polly saw Denise coming, she went the other way.

But this time Polly didn't back down. Why couldn't she have a turn? After all, Denise didn't own the monkey bars, even if she acted like she did.

"I don't see your name on them," Polly snapped back. She gave her body a hard swing, forcing Denise to step back. Then she flipped off the bars and landed upright, her feet hitting the ground with a satisfying *smack*.

Polly smiled to herself. She'd landed the cherry drop perfectly.

But Denise shrugged. "Cherry drops are for babies," she said. "I'm learning to do a *real* flip on my new trampoline at home."

Misty looked at her. "When did you get a trampoline?"

"My parents bought it last week. It's so much fun," Denise said. "*Way* better than this junky old playground equipment. We're also getting a hot tub, you know. Our backyard is huge, so we have plenty of room."

Polly scowled. She hated listening to Denise brag.

"You go ahead and play as long as you like," Denise told Polly in a sugary voice. "Your house is so small, school is

6

probably the only place where you get to have any fun."

Polly felt her cheeks get red. Ooh! Denise really burned her up! "It just so happens, I live in a mansion," she blurted out.

Denise snorted. "Yeah, right. I came to your first-grade birthday party, Polly. You live in that little white house on Pleasant Street. I'd hardly call that a mansion."

"That's my old house," Polly snapped. "My *new* house is much bigger. And we don't need a hot tub, because we have a *swimming pool*."

The little white house had been Polly's home before her dad married Veronica Kreep. After the wedding, her family had moved into the Kreeps' huge, spooky house. It was a mansion, but it wasn't exactly glamorous. It had a mossy roof, sagging shutters, and a creaky front door. And although there was a swimming pool, Polly had never put so much as a toe in its dark, slimy water. But Denise didn't need to know any of that.

"Actually, now that I think of it, I'm not sure it's a mansion. It might be a *castle*," Polly added. "It has towers, after all."

Polly was pleased to see a shadow of doubt flicker across Denise's face. "Towers?"

Polly nodded. "Two of them."

"I've never heard of a castle in Endsville." Denise tossed her curly brown hair. Then a sly look slid across her face. "Why don't we go to your house after school today, Polly? I've never been inside a castle before."

"Er, that's not . . . I d-d-don't think . . ." Polly stuttered. What had she done? Denise couldn't come over to her house and meet the Kreeps! She tried to think of an excuse, but her mind went blank.

8

"Great. Then it's all settled," Denise said. "We'll go over to your house — I mean, your *castle* — right after school." She snickered and, turning on her heel, she flounced away with her friend.

Just then, the bell rang. Recess was over. Polly headed for the school doors, feeling worried. She had to find a way out of this!

As she started inside, Mike fell into step beside her. "Hey, Polly, you missed a great game —"

"Mike!" Polly hissed, pulling him aside. "Denise wants to come over to my house after school!"

"Why'd you invite Denise over?" Mike asked. "I thought you couldn't stand her."

"I didn't invite her. She invited herself!" Polly twisted her fingers together worriedly. "Once Denise sees what the Kreeps are really like, she'll tell the whole school. What am I going to do?"

Polly had tried to keep what she knew about the Kreeps a secret — both for their sake and for hers. Mike was the only person she had told. "Maybe it won't be that bad. Just show her the normal parts of the house," he suggested.

Polly did a quick mental tour of her home. "*What* normal parts of the house?" she asked. This was going to be a disaster! Oh, if only she had a regular house like Mike's!

"That's it!" Polly exclaimed. "We can go to your house and pretend it's mine. Your parents usually aren't home after school. She'll never know the difference!" Mike's house wasn't a mansion, but it was on the largish side. *It just might work!* Polly thought.

But Mike shook his head. "Sorry, I can't help. I have soccer practice after school. Today's Friday, and we have that big tournament this weekend. I can't miss it."

Polly blew her hair out of her eyes and sighed. It looked like she was stuck — with Denise and the Kreeps.

⊰ Chapter 2 ⊱

Polly and Denise stood on the sidewalk in front of the Kreeps', staring up at the tall gray house. "*That's* where you live?" Denise asked.

Trying to look at it through Denise's eyes, Polly pretended she was seeing the house for the first time. She took in the dark windows, the peeling paint, and the two towers that jutted into the air like upside-down fangs. *You'd never know that eight people lived there,* Polly thought. *Not eight* living *people, anyway.*

"Well, I guess your house is big," Denise admitted grudgingly. "But it's definitely not a castle. What happened to your yard?" she asked, looking around at the weed-choked lawn. Polly's stepmother, Veronica, liked thistles and toadstools better than grass and flowers. But Polly wasn't about to tell Denise that.

"Er, the gardener has been away on vacation," she fibbed. "Well, now that you've seen it, I guess you probably have to go home." She began to steer Denise away. "See you Monday at school."

"Wait!" Denise dug in her heels. "I want to see the inside. And you have to show me your pool. *Remember?*"

Polly sighed. *How could I forget,* she thought. *Me and my big mouth.*

That afternoon, Polly had tried everything she could think of to get out of having

13

Denise over. She'd pretended to be sick, but the school nurse just took her temperature and sent her back to class. Then she'd talked in class without raising her hand, hoping that the teacher would keep her after school. But Mr. Crane had let her off with just a warning.

Just my luck, Polly thought. *The one day I actually want detention, I can't get it no matter how hard I try.*

"Isn't your mom going to be worried?" she asked Denise, stalling. "You never told her you were coming over."

"I already called her on my cell phone," Denise said. Her eyes narrowed suspiciously. "Why do I get the feeling you don't want to invite me in?"

Polly laughed nervously. "What gave you that idea?"

"I'll bet this isn't really your house, is it? You dragged me over to someone else's house, just so I'd think you live in a man-sion! That is so dumb, Polly."

"It is *so* my house!" Polly blurted angrily. "If you want to see it so badly, come on!" She turned on her heel and stomped up the front walkway. Denise followed close behind.

"Ew! What are those?" Denise squealed.

Polly turned. Denise was standing at the edge of the tangled flowerbed, pointing at one of the giant Venus flytraps that grew there.

"They're my stepmother's plants," Polly told her. "They're, um, a very exotic spe-cies." Polly decided not to mention that they were Venus flytraps. Normal families didn't grow flesh-eating plants in their flowerbeds.

"They're so ugly! They look like they have mouths." Denise leaned in and sniffed. "My mother grows roses. They smell heavenly.

15

But these don't smell like anything." She leaned even closer, still sniffing.

The plant's leaves started to move. Polly didn't think the flytraps ate people, but now wasn't the time to find out. She grabbed Denise and pulled her away just before the leaves closed on her nose.

Amazingly, Denise didn't notice. She was distracted by the dragon-shaped knocker on the front door. Its jaws were open in a horrible grimace.

Polly giggled nervously. "Er, Halloween decoration," she explained. As she pushed open the front door, its rusty hinges screamed.

Inside it was very dark compared to the bright day outside. Denise glanced around, taking in the cobwebs on the chandelier and the stone gargoyle at the end of the banister. "Wow, you guys decorated for Halloween really early this year."

Polly didn't correct her. It was better than Denise knowing the truth — that every day was Halloween at the Kreeps' house.

"Look at that one. It's so realistic!" Denise pointed to a hairy tarantula sitting on the stairs.

Polly's eyes widened. That spider wasn't just realistic — it was real! Bubbles the tarantula was her stepsister Esme's favorite pet.

Polly had to get Denise out of here before she realized the spider wasn't a fake. Normal families definitely didn't have tarantulas crawling around the house.

"Well, let's get this tour started!" she said brightly. "This is where we keep our coats!" Grabbing Denise, Polly pulled her into a coat closet and shut the door behind them.

The smell of wool and mothballs

17

settled over them. "It stinks in here," Denise complained. "Anyway, who cares where you keep your coats?" She started to reach for the door handle. Suddenly, she screamed.

Polly was so surprised, she screamed, too. When Polly screamed, Denise screamed again. The two girls tumbled out of the closet, screaming in unison.

"What? What is it?" Polly cried.

"I felt something furry brush against my leg!" Denise exclaimed.

Polly's blood turned cold. What had been in the closet with them? A giant mouse? Or a bat? Or something even worse? With the Kreeps, you never knew.

Polly turned to look, her heart pounding. As she did, a dark shape slipped from between the shoes on the closet floor.

"Oh, look. A little kitty!" Denise cried.

It was the little black cat with big green eyes that often appeared around the mansion. But like so many things in the Kreeps' house, the cat was more than what it seemed.

"Go on. Scram!" Polly told the cat. She didn't want it around while Denise was there. Polly suspected that the cat was really Esme, because it always appeared when the little girl *dis*appeared. The last thing Polly needed was Denise finding out about something like that.

The cat just flicked its tail. It gave Polly a resentful look.

"Cats love me," Denise told Polly. "I have two Persians, and they sleep on my bed every night. Here, kitty." She tried to grab it.

The cat hissed and swiped Denise with its claws.

"Ow!" Denise pulled her hand back. "It scratched me!"

"Now see what you've done?" Polly told the cat. "Get out of here! And take Bubbles with you."

Denise frowned. "Who's Bubbles?"

"It's just — um, her cat toy. Are you okay?" Polly examined Denise's hand.

"I guess so." Denise sniffed. "You should get your cat declawed if it's going to scratch people like — oh!" Denise started and stared.

Polly turned. Esme was standing behind her. The little girl had on a black dress, and her black hair was pulled into two pigtails. She glared darkly at Denise.

Denise turned to Polly. "Who's that?"

"Esme, my stepsister," Polly told her.

"She just appeared out of nowhere!" Denise said.

"Ha-ha." Polly pretended to laugh, but her knees were shaking. What had Denise seen? "Esme, say hi to Denise," she instructed, trying to keep her voice calm.

"*Sssss*," Esme hissed.

"Don't mind her. She, uh, likes to pretend she's a cat," Polly said, pulling Denise away. "Anyway, let's get on with the tour."

"Aren't we going to have a snack?" Denise asked as they walked down the narrow hallway. "I always get a snack when I get home from school."

"Of course!" Polly led the way to the kitchen. Like the rest of the house, it was dark and gloomy. *But at least there isn't anything too weird there*, Polly thought as she turned the corner.

She stopped in her tracks. A cauldron big enough to poach a pumpkin in was sitting in the middle of the kitchen floor. Polly's stepmother, Veronica, was standing over it, stirring.

"Hello, dear," Veronica said pleasantly. "Did you just get home from —"

Slam! Polly shut the kitchen door and whirled to face Denise, hoping she hadn't seen anything. "I just remembered!" she told Denise quickly. "I have some peanut butter crackers up in my room. Let's go there instead."

As they headed toward the stairs, Denise glanced out a window that overlooked the backyard. "Oh, is that the pool?" she asked. "Let me see it!"

The last thing Polly wanted to do was show Denise the pool. But she didn't know what to say. She led Denise outside.

"Why is the water all murky?" Denise asked when they got to the pool. "Don't you use chlorine?"

"Chlorine is, um, really bad for your skin," Polly replied. She peered nervously into the water, hoping that Mutt didn't pick this moment to come to the surface. Mutt was the thing that lived in the pool. Nobody was sure what Mutt was, not even the Kreeps.

"I guess you weren't lying about having a pool," Denise said grudgingly. "Well, let's go swimming!"

"Swimming?" Polly asked, horrified.

"That *is* what you do in a pool," Denise sneered.

"B-but we can't go in there!" Polly stuttered.

"Why not?" Denise asked.

Goose bumps sprang up on Polly's arms. Just the thought of climbing into that dark water gave her the chills. "Because, um . . . it's too cold out to swim."

"No, it's not. It's a beautiful day." Denise frowned. "Are you *shivering*?"

A few bubbles had appeared on the mucky surface of the pool. "Come on. Let's go play in my room," Polly pleaded, trying to pull Denise along.

Denise shook her hand off. "There's something funny going on. You've been acting weird ever since we got here," she said, her eyes narrowing suspiciously.

Polly gulped. How much had Denise figured out?

"You know what I think? I think . . ." Denise's voice trailed off. She was staring at something behind Polly.

Polly turned. A tall figure in a dark, hooded sweatshirt had emerged from the house. It glided smoothly across the cement patio. A low wall at the edge of the patio hid the figure's feet. From where Polly and

Denise were standing, it looked like it was floating.

"Who is *that*?" Denise whispered.

"My stepbrother Vincent," said Polly.

They watched as Vincent hopped up and over the wall on his skateboard. As Vincent landed, his hood fell back, revealing his pale face and bright green eyes. Without stopping, he glided over the grass and disappeared around the corner of the house.

Denise hadn't taken her eyes from him. "I've never seen anyone ride a skateboard over grass before," she murmured.

"Well, Vincent has a, er, *special* talent," Polly answered quickly. She had always suspected that her oldest stepbrother could fly, although she had never been able to prove it. But to Polly there was no other explanation for some of Vincent's skateboarding tricks.

Denise had turned slightly pale. Polly could only imagine what she was thinking. It was time to get Denise out of the house, before something even worse happened.

"Oh, my gosh!" Polly exclaimed. "Look at the time! I promised my stepmother I would help her garden the weeds . . . I mean, weed the garden!"

Denise didn't answer. She still was staring after Vincent, looking a little dazed.

Polly gulped. Why did she have that strange expression on her face? Had Vincent scared her *that* much? "Denise, you should probably go," Polly said, a little louder.

"What?" Denise blinked at her. "Oh. Okay."

Polly didn't want to risk another trip through the house, so she led her around the side. Denise followed quietly. Her silence made Polly nervous.

"Well, thanks for coming over," she said when they reached the sidewalk.

Denise just nodded and started off down the street, still looking dazed.

As soon as she was gone, Polly raced back into the house. She slammed the door behind her, then leaned against it and blew her bangs out of her eyes.

That was horrible, Polly thought. Denise had clearly been shocked. By Monday, everyone at school would know all about Polly's crazy family.

Still, she thought, *there is one bright side. Denise is sure never going to come back.*

❋ Chapter 3 ❋

Polly woke early the next morning. It was Saturday, but she could never sleep late in this old house. There were too many noises — the sounds of mice scuttling across wood floors, or bats returning home after a night of hunting.

Polly lay in bed thinking about Denise's visit the day before. Could she possibly have believed that Polly's house was decorated for Halloween? And what about the odd encounter with Vincent? Every time Polly thought of the strange expression on Denise's face, she felt like hiding under her covers.

Still, today was a new day. If her life was going to be over on Monday, she might as well enjoy the weekend.

Polly climbed out of bed and lifted her curtains to check the weather. Rain lashed against the glass. She opened the window and stuck her head out. It was the same everywhere: rain, rain, rain.

She sighed. The weekend was sure getting off to a bad start.

Polly got dressed and went downstairs to breakfast. Veronica, Esme, and Polly's dad were gathered around the kitchen table.

"Good morning, dear," Veronica said. "Beautiful day, isn't it?"

"Every day that we're all together is a beautiful one," Polly's dad agreed, patting Veronica's hand.

Polly rolled her eyes. "It's raining cats and dogs," she complained.

"It *is*?" Esme hurried over to the window to look.

"You know why you have to watch out when it's raining cats and dogs?" Polly's dad asked.

Polly knew what was coming: a corny joke. Her dad was famous for them. "Why do you have to watch out?" she asked, already starting to smile.

"So you don't step in a poodle!"

"Ha-ha!" Polly's older sister, Joy, laughed as she walked into the room. "Good one, Dad."

"No practice today?" her dad asked, noticing Joy's jeans and sweatshirt. Joy was a cheerleader at Endsville High. Her team usually practiced on Saturday mornings.

"We have the day off." Joy poured a glass of juice, then turned to Polly and Esme.

"Hey, guys, I was thinking the three of us could hang out today. You know, do some big-sister, little-sister stuff. It will be really fun! What do you say?"

"Um, gosh, I wish I could. But I have a lot of homework," Polly fibbed. She liked her older sister. But Joy's idea of fun was mostly . . . well, *cheerleading*.

"What about you, Esme?" Joy said, turning. She looked around. "Where did she go? She was right here!"

Out of the corner of her eye, Polly saw a little black cat slinking toward the door. *Clever Esme*, she thought. Cheerleading clearly wasn't Esme's idea of fun, either.

But Veronica smiled. "Joy, what a nice idea," she said. "I'm sure Esme would love to spend the day with her big sister!"

From the other room, there came a loud yowl of protest.

31

"Gosh!" said Polly's dad, looking up in surprise. "I wonder what's wrong with the cat?"

Later that morning, Polly lounged in one of the bat-shaped chairs in the living room. A library book sat open in her lap, but she wasn't reading. There was too much noise to concentrate.

"Give me an *S*!" Joy yelled as she threw her arms in the air. "Give me a *P*! Give me an *I – R – I – T*! What's that spell?"

Esme stood at Joy's side, holding a pompom in one hand and Bubbles the tarantula in the other. For the past hour, Joy had been trying to teach her a cheer.

"I said, *What's that spell?*" Joy boomed.

"'Spirit!'" their brother, Petey, hollered from the other room.

"Okay! Now try it again, Esme!" Joy instructed. "Give me an S!"

"*Sssssss!*" the little girl hissed.

"Not bad!" Joy said encouragingly. "Try again, with a little more *smile!*"

Polly could say one thing for Joy: she never gave up. *Poor Esme*, Polly thought.

"Hey, I have an idea," she said, standing up. "Why don't we play a game instead?"

"I thought you had homework," said Joy.

Polly shrugged. "I can do it later."

"I know a game," said Esme, brightening. "Snakes and Ladders!" She ran to a cabinet in the corner of the room and pulled out a dusty cardboard box. As she took off the lid, something long and black slithered out of the box and disappeared into a crack in the wall.

"Rats," said Esme. "Now we're missing a piece."

"That's okay," said Polly quickly. "We can play a different game instead. How about charades?"

"Ooh! Can I go first?" Joy bounced up and down.

"Okay," Polly and Esme said, nodding.

"Here's the clue." Joy scratched her head with one hand. With the other hand she scratched her armpit.

Esme giggled. "You look like Cousin Alfred!" she said.

"Wrong!" said Joy. "Guess again." She swelled her chest and pounded it with both fists.

Just then, Vincent walked into the room. "What's wrong with Joy?" he asked Polly and Esme.

"We're playing charades," Polly told him.

"Oh," said Vincent. "For a minute I

thought that cheerleading had finally destroyed all her brain cells."

Joy ignored him. She pretended to pick a bug out of Polly's hair and eat it.

"We're supposed to guess what Joy is," Esme explained to her older brother.

"That's easy," said Vincent. "Cousin Alfred."

Joy frowned. She crouched down and walked around the room, dragging her knuckles.

"You look just like him. Mother! Damon!" Vincent called into the other room. "Come in here. You've got to see this!"

Veronica and Damon came into the living room, followed by Dr. Winkler and Petey. They all stared at Joy, who was now jumping up and down on the couch.

"Who does Joy remind you of?" Vincent asked them.

"Cousin Alfred!" said Damon.

Veronica nodded. "The spitting image."

"Who is Cousin Alfred?" Polly's dad asked.

"He wasn't at the wedding, dear," Veronica told him. "He couldn't get away from work. He's a stockbroker — very busy."

Joy sighed and dropped her arms. "I give up. I was *supposed* to be a gorilla," she said, climbing down off the couch.

"I never would have guessed that," said Damon.

"Are you playing charades?" asked Polly's dad. "I'll take a turn!"

The rest of the family took seats around the room. "Ready?" said Dr. Winkler. "Okay. Here's the clue." He began to circle the room in a stiff-legged walk. His feet thudded with every step.

"A zombie!" guessed Esme.

"A football player!" guessed Joy.

Dr. Winkler rolled his eyes. "Rrrrrr," he groaned dramatically.

Polly giggled. Her dad looked really funny. The rest of the family was laughing, too.

"I know!" Petey shouted. "Frankenstein!"

"No, no!" Veronica cried. "Uncle Frank!"

Dr. Winkler dropped his pose. "Actually, I *was* supposed to be Frankenstein."

Veronica smiled. "Well, I was close! This game is fun. May I take a turn?"

As she stood up, a sound like a lion's roar echoed through the house. It was the mansion's doorbell.

"I'll get it," said Polly, hopping up.

She hurried into the front hallway. She could hear the rest of the family laughing in the other room. "Don't start without

37

me!" Polly called to them, reaching for the door handle.

She yanked open the door — and froze.

Denise Dunleavy was standing on the front steps.

❊ Chapter 4 ❊

Polly stared, hardly able to believe her eyes. Denise was wearing pink rubber rain boots. Rain dripped off the hood of her pretty white raincoat. *This must be a nightmare*, Polly told herself. *A nightmare in a white coat and pink galoshes.*

"I was in the neighborhood so I thought I'd drop by," Denise told Polly. "Aren't you going to invite me in?"

"Polly? Who is it?" Veronica came gliding down the hallway. "Hello," she said when she saw Denise. "Are you a friend of Polly's? Why don't you come inside?"

"Thanks, I will," said Denise, pushing past her.

In the hallway, Denise shrugged out of her coat. "Use a wooden hanger, please," she said, tossing the wet slicker to Polly. "I hate wire hangers."

"We're just in the middle of a game," Veronica told Denise.

"I'm good at games," Denise said. Without waiting for Polly, she followed Veronica into the living room.

For a moment, Polly was too stunned to move. She stared at the coat in her hands. Then, tossing it onto the stone gargoyle's head, she hurried after Denise.

By the time Polly got to the living room, Denise was already seated on the couch next to Vincent. "I'm really good at cha-rades," Denise was saying. "My mother says I could be an actress. Do you think I'd make a good movie star?"

Vincent shrugged.

Damon tugged Polly aside. "What's *she* doing here?" he hissed. Denise and Damon were enemies at school.

"I have no idea!" Polly whispered back.

"Okay, everyone ready? It's Veronica's turn!" Joy announced.

Please don't do anything too weird, Veronica, Polly pleaded silently. With Denise watching, the game didn't seem fun anymore.

Veronica crouched down. She began to sniff the air.

"A bear," guessed Petey.

"Someone with a head cold!" guessed Polly's dad.

Veronica bared her teeth. Suddenly, she tipped her head back and howled up at the sky, "Arooooo!"

"A wolf!" Denise yelled. At the same moment Damon cried, "Great-Grandma Bogdana!"

"Correct!" exclaimed Veronica, straightening up.

Denise frowned. "Which one's correct?"

"Both of you," Veronica said, smiling pleasantly.

Denise put her hands on her hips. "That's dumb!" she scoffed. "How can someone's grandma be the same as a wolf?"

Polly could think of a way — if the Kreeps' great-grandma *was* a wolf — a werewolf, to be exact! The last thing she needed was Denise knowing something like that!

"Whose turn is it next?" Polly asked quickly, hoping to change the subject.

But Denise wouldn't let it go. "I want to know who's right, me or Damon?" she demanded.

"Believe me," Polly murmured, "you don't want to know."

"Well, I think I've had enough games for now. Who wants lunch?" Veronica asked brightly.

"Oh! Me! I do!" The rest of the family leaped up and headed toward the dining room.

"Would you like to stay for lunch?" Veronica asked Denise.

"No, she can't —" Polly began.

"I'd love to!" Denise interrupted.

Polly groaned inwardly. What *was* Denise doing here? And why wouldn't she leave?

Moments later, the Winklers, the Kreeps, and Denise all gathered around the long dining room table.

"That's *my* chair," Esme said as Denise slid into the seat next to Vincent.

"Scram, pip-squeak," Denise muttered. "*I'm* the guest here."

Esme's big green eyes flashed angrily. But Denise didn't notice. She was too busy smiling at Vincent. "So, what is your favorite food?" she asked.

Vincent glanced at her. "Meat."

"Me, too!" Denise told him. "I love a really good — *yeowch*!" She screamed and scrambled out of her chair. "Something bit me!"

Everyone looked under the table. A little black cat with big green eyes was crouched there. It glared up at Denise.

"Naughty kitty," Veronica said, scooping it up. She gently set it outside the door, saying, "Come back when you're ready to behave."

44

"Now," Veronica said, returning to the table. "Casserole?" She passed a plate to Denise.

Polly tensed. A rubbery tentacle dangled from the side of the plate. Veronica's cooking was always weird, and today was no exception.

But Denise barely glanced at the food. "I'd prefer something fresh, if you don't mind," she told Veronica. "Maybe a nice salad with some grilled tuna and mango-lime dressing. Do you have anything like that?"

Veronica looked at her coldly. "Sorry," she said. "We're *fresh* out." Not many things bothered Veronica. But Polly could tell Denise had definitely rubbed her the wrong way.

Polly's dad cleared his throat. "Hey, that reminds me of a joke. How do you fix a broken tomato?"

"Oh, that's an old one," Denise told him. "The answer is 'tomato paste.'"

"That's right," said Dr. Winkler with a slight frown. He looked disappointed.

"You know," Joy said brightly, getting up from the table, "I could really go for a smoothie. Do you want me to make you one, too, Denise? That's nice and fresh, right?"

"With soy milk, please." Denise sniffed.

"I'll see what we have." Joy disappeared into the kitchen.

"So," Denise said, turning back to Vincent, "I hear you like skateboarding."

"Hnnh," Vincent grunted. He had his head down close to his plate and was shoveling in bites of the rubbery casserole. Polly watched her teenage stepbrother with disgust. *He's such an animal!* she thought. She wondered why Denise kept talking to him.

"Here we are!" Joy swept back into the room carrying two pink smoothies. "Strawberry surprise — my specialty!"

"Better watch out," Vincent told Denise. "You never know what she put in there. Joy's got pom-poms for brains."

Joy ignored him. She was used to his jokes about cheerleading. But Denise burst out laughing. "Pom-poms for brains!" she screeched. "Oh, that's so funny. Pom-poms for brains. Ha-ha-ha!"

Joy's sunny smile faded. She slammed the smoothie down in front of Denise and stalked back to her seat. *Wow*, Polly thought. *Denise even made Joy mad. That's almost impossible!*

Vincent scraped the last of his lunch off his plate. Then he pushed back his chair.

"Where are you going?" Veronica asked.

Vincent shrugged. "Out," he said simply.

He flipped his hood up over his pale face and slunk out of the room.

"Teenagers," said Veronica, shaking her head.

Denise pushed her chair back and stood up. "I'm finished, too."

"But you haven't even touched your smoothie," Polly pointed out.

Denise shrugged. "I guess I'm not hungry. Let's go play in your room."

Polly would rather have stayed with the rest of her family. But from the way they were all glaring at Denise, she knew it was time to get her out of there.

As they made their way up the stairs to Polly's room, Polly relaxed for the first time. As far as she was concerned, her room was the only truly normal part of the house. When Denise saw it, maybe she'd realize that Polly wasn't so weird after all.

"Here's my room," Polly said proudly, pushing open the door.

But Denise barely glanced twice at Polly's room. She just pushed aside a pile of stuffed animals and plopped down on the bed. "Where did Vincent go?" she asked.

Polly picked up a stuffed bunny that had fallen on the floor. "Skateboarding, probably." She decided not to mention that Vincent's favorite place to skateboard was the town cemetery.

Denise twirled a curl around her finger. "Does he have a girlfriend?"

"No. At least, not that I know of." Polly had never thought about Vincent with a girlfriend. *More like a ghoul-friend*, she thought with a giggle.

"Does he go to Endsville High?" Denise wanted to know.

Why is she asking so many questions

49

about Vincent? Polly wondered, looking at her curiously. Denise was staring into space with a dreamy expression.

"You like Vincent!" Polly realized with a gasp. Why hadn't she seen it before? That was why Denise had shown up again today, and why she kept hanging around. She had a crush on Polly's stepbrother!

"He's soooo cute." Denise sighed.

Vincent? Cute? "He's fourteen," Polly told Denise. "He's too old for you. And anyway, Vincent's not so great," she added. "He's got some, er, strange hobbies."

"I know, like *skateboarding*," said Denise. "It's hard to believe that toad Damon has such a cool older brother! So, do you think he likes me?"

Polly didn't know how to answer. She didn't think Vincent had even noticed

Denise. "You two really don't have much in common," she pointed out.

"Opposites attract," Denise said, hopping up from the bed. "Promise me you'll find out what he thinks about me, Polly?"

It was the last thing Polly wanted to do. But she was willing to say anything to get Denise out of her hair. Crossing her fingers behind her back, she gave a tiny nod.

"Great!" Denise got up and went to the door. Polly followed her back downstairs.

"Remember, you promised," Denise said as she put on her coat at the front door.

"Yep," said Polly. She hustled Denise out the door and slammed it behind her. *Phew!* Polly thought. *At least that's over.*

Denise called something through the door.

"What did you say?" Polly shouted back.

"I said" — Denise's voice sounded muffled — "see you tomorrow!"

Polly gulped. *Tomorrow?*

✳ Chapter 5 ❦

Later that afternoon, Polly sat in her room. She stared at the rain pelting the window.

Why, oh, why did Denise have to like Vincent, Polly wondered. Couldn't she see that they were nothing alike? All Denise cared about was having the fanciest house and the best clothes. And all Vincent cared about was — well, Polly wasn't sure what he cared about, but she knew it wasn't stuff like that.

Just thinking about Denise and Vincent was starting to give Polly a headache.

She knew she had to end Denise's crush. But how?

She reached for the phone to call Mike, then stopped. Mike didn't know a thing about crushes or romance. Polly was pretty sure of that. But who else could she ask?

"Knock, knock." Joy's cheerful voice rang out as she pushed open the door and walked into Polly's room. She was carrying an armful of clothes. "I was just weeding out my closet," she told Polly. "I wondered if you wanted any of these old cheerleading uniforms."

"What for?" asked Polly.

"What for?" Joy's big blue eyes blinked. "For when you become a cheerleader, silly!"

Polly sighed. Becoming a cheerleader was the last thing on her mind right now.

Joy sat down next to her. "Is something wrong?"

Polly wondered if she should tell her sister. Joy had had boyfriends before. *And she's probably had crushes, too*, thought Polly. Maybe Joy could tell her how to cure Denise's crush.

"I think I need some advice," she said finally.

Joy's face lit up. "Really? Okay, first, you need a haircut. You can't cheer with your bangs hanging in your eyes like that. Next, we should probably work on your cartwheel —"

"Wait," Polly cut her off. "I didn't mean about cheerleading. I was talking about Denise."

"Oh." Joy frowned. "To be perfectly honest, Polly, she doesn't seem like much of a cheerleader to me."

Polly shook her head. "That's not what I —"

"Frankly, she's more the drill team type," Joy added with a sniff. "Not that there's anything wrong with that."

Polly sighed. Joy wasn't going to be much help, after all. "Thanks, Joy. I'll tell her."

After Joy had left, Polly went back to staring out the window. She wondered if she should talk to her dad. But that seemed too embarrassing. Just thinking about boys and crushes made Polly's face turn red.

Polly didn't want to tell Vincent about Denise's crush. And she knew Petey, Damon, and Esme wouldn't be able to help.

That left Veronica.

Polly found her stepmother in the kitchen. She was standing with her back to Polly, stirring the cauldron from the day before.

"Come in, Polly," Veronica said without turning around.

Polly shivered. It always spooked her, how Veronica seemed to have eyes in the back of her head. "What are you doing?" she asked nervously.

"Oh, this is just a little hobby of mine," Veronica told her. "Come take a look."

Polly crept closer. The liquid in the pot was dark purple and had a funny smell. *What is in there?* Polly wondered. *Snake poison? Bat's blood?*

Polly held her breath as Veronica reached into the pot with a pair of tongs and pulled out . . .

"A T-shirt?" Polly asked in surprise.

Veronica laughed. "Of course! What did you think it would be?"

Polly shook her head, too embarrassed to say.

"I'm tie-dyeing," Veronica explained. She dropped the shirt back into the pot, then turned to a rack in the corner. Clothes with delicate spiderweb designs were spread out to dry. "I finished those yesterday."

Polly thought back to the day before, when she'd rushed Denise away from the kitchen. Veronica hadn't been doing anything witchy after all.

Maybe Dad and Joy and Petey are right. Maybe I do have a big imagination, Polly thought with a sigh.

Veronica rinsed her hands and dried them on a towel. "I can see you didn't come to talk about crafts. What's on your mind?"

"Well," Polly said hesitantly. "I have this friend, and she likes, er, this boy."

"Oh?" Veronica's thin eyebrows arched. "When did this start?"

"Yesterday," Polly said.

Veronica sat down at the table, and Polly sat across from her. "I see," Veronica said thoughtfully. "Love is a powerful emotion, Polly."

"I didn't say *love*," Polly put in quickly. "It's more of a crush."

"Love can be crushing," Veronica agreed. "Love is like a great big python. It squeezes your heart like a small defenseless frog, then swallows it whole."

Ugh. Polly shuddered. *Veronica sure has a way with words.* "So how do you get rid of it?" she asked.

"Goodness!" Veronica blinked at her in surprise. "Why would you want to do that?"

"Well, what if you have a crush on . . . the wrong person? Isn't there something that can make it go away? Like a charm . . . or a potion or something?" she added slyly.

Veronica was quiet for a moment. Polly's heart sped up. It was the closest she had ever come to suggesting that Veronica was really a witch. Would her stepmother be angry?

But Veronica just sighed. "When it comes to love," she said at last, "it's better to let things take care of themselves."

Let things take care of themselves? What does that *mean?* Polly waited for her stepmother to go on. But Veronica's mind seemed to be elsewhere. She went over to the cauldron and gave the clothes a thoughtful stir.

Polly stood up. It seemed like that was all she was going to get from Veronica. No charm, no potion. Just some advice that wasn't even helpful.

Well, thought Polly, *it looks like I'm on my own.*

✢ Chapter 6 ✢

Sunday morning, Polly was in her room when a loud noise echoed through the house.

ROAR! ROAR! ROARRRRR! Someone was leaning on the doorbell.

Polly went downstairs to answer it. But the rest of the family had the same idea. They all arrived at the door at once.

Dr. Winkler laughed. "How many people does it take to answer a door?" he joked as he pulled the door open.

For a second, Polly didn't recognize the hooded figure standing on the doorstep. Then a familiar, sneering voice said, "What

61

are you staring at? Aren't you going to invite me in?"

It was Denise! But she looked completely different. Her white coat and pink boots were gone. Instead, she was wearing black jeans and a black windbreaker with the hood pulled up. Even her nail polish was black! Denise looked taller than usual, too. Polly looked down and saw she was wearing in-line skates.

Suddenly, Polly understood. *She's trying to impress Vincent. Right down to the wheels on her feet!*

"I thought we should go skating today," Denise told Polly. She wobbled a little as she tried to balance.

"But I don't have skates," Polly told her.

"Too bad. Would anyone *else* like to come with me?" Denise asked, looking at Vincent.

"Nope."

"Not me."

"Busy, gotta run."

"Do I smell something burning?"

The entire family scattered, leaving Polly alone with Denise.

"So?" Denise hissed, clutching at Polly's arm. "Did you find out if Vincent likes me?"

"I didn't really get a chance to ask him," Polly said.

"Can't you do anything right?" Denise snapped. "I guess I'm going to have to handle this myself."

Still wobbling, Denise skated down the hallway to the living room. Vincent was lying on the sofa, looking through the newspaper.

"Hi, Vincent." Denise grabbed on to the end of the couch to steady herself. "What are you reading?"

"I'm seeing what movies are playing," Vincent muttered.

"I love movies!" Denise squealed. "What are you going to see?"

Vincent mumbled something behind the newspaper. It sounded like "Tiffany's."

"Did you say *Breakfast at Tiffany's*?" Denise gave a little hop of excitement and almost fell over. "That's my favorite movie! Tiffany's is this really expensive jewelry store — my mom has earrings from there, you know — and, well . . . Anyway, it's a super-romantic movie. I'd love to see it again."

She paused, waiting.

Vincent turned a page.

With a quick jerk, Denise yanked the paper from his hands. "I *said*, I'd *love* to see it again!" she repeated.

Polly sucked in her breath. No one ever bossed Vincent around like that. She had no idea what he would do.

Vincent stared at Denise for a

moment. Then he shrugged. "So why don't you?" he replied. "It's playing at the Cineplex."

"Ooh! You're so sweet for asking," Denise squealed. "I'd love to go!"

Vincent rode his skateboard. Denise skated. Polly didn't want to leave Denise alone with Vincent, so she rode her bike. She wasn't sure if she was more worried about Denise or her stepbrother. All she knew was that something bad was bound to happen.

Denise wasn't a very good skater, and Polly had to ride slowly. By the time they got to the movie theater, they had lost sight of Vincent. "We must have beaten him here," Denise said. She hurried over to the ticket window. "Two for *Tiffany's*, please."

At least she's buying my ticket, Polly thought. *That's the first nice thing Denise has ever done.*

But as Polly started to follow her into the theater, Denise blocked her way. "You can go home now," she said.

"What?" Polly asked, startled.

"Didn't you see the way Vincent looked at me? I think he really likes me," Denise told her.

"Are you sure you want to go to the movies with him alone?" Polly asked.

Denise rolled her eyes. "Haven't you heard the expression, 'Two's company, three's a crowd'? I came here on a date with Vincent. And *you're* crowding us, Polly."

"Then why did you buy me a ticket?" Polly wondered.

"This ticket isn't for you. It's for Vincent," Denise said. She looked down the street. "I wonder what's taking him so long."

Just then, Vincent stuck his head out the door of the theater. "What's taking you guys so long?" he asked.

"I got you a ticket!" Denise purred, waving it in the air.

"I already got a ticket," Vincent said. "I saved you both seats, but you'd better hurry. The movie's about to start." He disappeared back inside.

Denise scowled at the ticket in her hand. Then she shoved it at Polly. "By the way," she said as they went in, "you owe me five dollars for that."

Inside the theater, Denise made sure to get a seat next to Vincent. Polly sat on the aisle. As the lights dimmed, Denise turned to Polly. "Could you go get some popcorn?"

"Get it yourself," Polly said. She didn't want to miss the previews. They were her favorite part of going to the movies. Besides,

67

she was getting tired of Denise's bossy attitude.

"But *you're* on the aisle," Denise whined. "And if I try to skate in the dark, I might break a leg or something."

Polly didn't say anything. Maybe if she just ignored her, Denise would stop talking.

No such luck. "*Come on*, Polly." Denise poked her. "You owe me for the ticket."

"Oh, all right," Polly snapped. She trudged up the aisle. By the time she got back with the popcorn, the previews were over.

Great, Polly thought unhappily. She sat down just as the movie title came up on the screen. *Gorefest at Tiffany's*, it read. Blood dripped from the letters. This wasn't a romance, Polly realized. It was a horror film!

Denise turned to Vincent. "You said this was *Breakfast at Tiffany's*!"

Vincent shook his head. "I didn't say that. *You* did."

"Hmph." Denise folded her arms and frowned. Then a sly look crossed her face. Polly could see it even in the dark.

"If I get scared," Denise told Vincent, "you'll have to put your arm around me."

Oh, brother, Polly thought, rolling her eyes. Denise noticed her and scowled. "You forgot to get butter!" she snapped, thrusting the popcorn back at Polly.

This time, Polly didn't mind going to the snack stand. She didn't like horror movies very much. Living with the Kreeps was spooky enough.

She took her time getting butter. When she got back to the theater, Denise was scrunched down in her seat.

"Here's the popcorn," said Polly.

Denise took the bag without a word. Her eyes were glued to the screen, where a pack of zombies were chasing a man around a jewelry store. Vincent seemed to think the movie was funny. He laughed a lot. But Denise didn't seem to be enjoying it much. Every time something scary happened, she covered her eyes.

"Hey, you aren't eating the popcorn," Polly whispered, poking her.

"Yahhhh!" Denise shrieked. The popcorn went flying.

"Never mind," Polly said, getting up from her seat. "I'll get more."

Polly missed most of the second half of the film. She was too scared to watch. Finally, she heard Vincent say, "You can take your hands off your eyes now."

Polly peeped through her fingers. The lights were on. People were exiting

70

the movie theater. But Denise was still scrunched down in her seat. Her hands were gripping the armrests, and her eyes were squeezed shut.

"It's over, Denise," Polly told her.

Denise cracked one eye open. "It is?"

"So?" said Vincent. "What did you think?"

"I . . . er . . . absolutely loved it!" Denise gushed.

Polly shook her head. At least the movie was over. But she was still in the dark about Vincent and Denise. How would *that* scary story end?

⚜ Chapter 7 ⚜

Wow!" Vincent said as they exited the theater. "I haven't seen a comedy that good in years."

Denise shivered. "I didn't think it was very funny."

"Are you kidding?" Vincent said. "Of course it was funny. Real zombies aren't anything like that!"

Polly didn't want to ask how Vincent knew so much about "real" zombies. Denise didn't say anything, either. She looked a little green. *Good*, thought Polly. *Maybe this "date" is finally over.* "I guess you probably have to go home now, don't you, Denise?" she asked as she unlocked her bike.

"You can't go home yet!" said Vincent. "I thought we could go to Lookout Point."

"Lookout Point?" asked Denise, brightening.

Polly groaned inwardly. Lookout Point was the most romantic spot in Endsville. From the top of the hill there was a beautiful view of the city. *Why would Vincent want to go to Lookout Point?* she wondered. *Unless . . .*

Unless he really likes Denise, Polly thought, answering her own question.

With a sinking feeling, Polly looked from Vincent to Denise. In their black hooded jackets, they looked a lot alike. *Maybe they have more in common than I thought,* she mused.

"Well, come on!" Denise cried. All the

color had come back into her cheeks. "What are we waiting for?"

A short time later, they were climbing the winding road to Lookout Point. "Are you sure about this?" Polly asked Denise as she slowly pedaled up the steep hill.

"Sure . . . I'm . . . sure," Denise panted. She was inching along in her skates. "This . . . is . . . so . . . romantic."

Finally, she stopped to catch her breath. "Vincent makes it look so easy," she said, gazing at him dreamily.

Ahead of them, Vincent was gliding gracefully uphill on his skateboard. He seemed to be going against gravity.

Show-off, Polly thought. She wished Vincent would try a little harder to keep his supernatural powers secret. "This hill *is* really steep. Maybe we should just go back down," she said to Denise.

"I have a better idea. You can pull me up the hill," Denise said.

Pedaling up the hill with Denise holding on to her bike was twice as hard. Especially with Denise shouting, "Can't you go any faster?"

By the time Polly got to the top, she was exhausted.

Denise, on the other hand, wasn't even short of breath. "Oh, how pretty!" she sighed, admiring the view. "Vincent, aren't you going to come over here and look?"

"I'm looking at it," said Vincent from the other side of the hill.

"But the city is this way," Denise told him.

"Who cares about the city?" Vincent said. "*That's* what I'm talking about."

Polly and Denise gazed where he was

75

pointing. On the back side of Lookout Hill was a single steep narrow street that went straight down to the bottom.

"That's the steepest road in Endsville. It's a beastly ride down," Vincent said.

"You're not going down that?" Denise asked in horror.

"No, *we're* going down it," said Vincent.

Denise turned pale. Vincent laughed. "Why did you think we came up here?" he asked.

Denise didn't say anything. She looked too frightened to talk. Polly couldn't really blame her. She didn't want to go down that crazy hill, either.

"All right," said Vincent. "Who's going first?"

"Er . . . why don't *you* go first, Vincent?" Polly suggested. "Show us how it's done."

"Good idea," said Vincent. He stepped onto his board, pushed the ground twice, and took off, flying down the hill. For a moment, he was just a blur.

He's going fast! thought Polly.

At the bottom, he came to a graceful stop, then turned and called up to Polly and Denise. "Who's next?"

The two girls looked at each other.

"Y-you go," Denise stuttered. "I want to enjoy the view a little longer."

Polly tightened the chin strap on her bicycle helmet. Then she inched her bike forward and peered down the hill. The road was steep, but it was straight and smooth. As long as she didn't hit a rock or something, she'd be okay.

Polly was about to push off when Vincent suddenly yelled, "Wait!"

Polly's heart leaped. "What's wrong?"

Vincent pulled a small digital camera from his pocket. "I want to get this on film!" He switched the camera on. "Okay! Go!"

Polly took a deep breath. It was now or never. She pushed off, and suddenly she was zooming down the hill. The wind stung her cheeks. Faster and faster — she felt like she was flying!

A second later, she screeched to a stop next to Vincent. Her hands shook from gripping the handlebars.

"I did it!" Polly cried excitedly. "I did it!" The ride had been thrilling — scary and fun, all at once.

"Deadly cool," Vincent said with a nod.

Polly beamed. She'd never gotten a compliment from Vincent before. She turned and called up the hill, "Your turn, Denise!"

Denise stood at the edge, looking down. "I think there's something wrong with my skates," she yelled. "I'm just going to walk —"

She didn't finish the sentence. Her Rollerblades slid out from under her, and she went whizzing down the hill.

"Aaaaaaaaah!" Denise screamed and flapped her arms up and down. She looked like she was trying to fly.

"You've got it!" Polly cried. "Just watch out for that —"

Denise slammed into a bush. She spun all the way around once. But somehow she managed to stay on her feet.

"Aaaaaaah!" she screamed.

"Tree branch, dead ahead!" Polly shouted.

Denise tried to duck beneath it, but it was too late. She caught the branch, swinging on it like a trapeze artist. When she let go, she was skating backward, her rear end leading the way. Her arms flapped and flailed.

"Watch out!" Polly tried to get out of the way. "Watch out! Watch out! Watch —"

Crash! Denise smacked into her. They both tumbled to the ground.

"Ow," Polly grunted. Denise was sitting on top of her.

"Aaaaah!" Denise wailed. "I almost died! That was . . . that was . . ."

"Brilliant," said Vincent.

"It was?" Denise stopped crying.

"Wow, this is truly priceless." Vincent was watching the video on his camera screen.

"It is? I mean, I'm sure it is." Denise wobbled to her feet and patted her curls into place. "After all, my mother says I'm a natural athlete."

Oh, no, thought Polly. *Here we go again.* "It's getting pretty late," she said. She stood up and brushed herself off. "We'd better go home."

"Not yet," Vincent said, putting the camera back in his pocket. "There's still one more place I want to take you."

"Where's that?" asked Denise. She sounded a little nervous.

"The pet shop. It's right on the way home." Vincent climbed onto his skateboard.

"Pet shop?" Denise squealed. "I *love* animals."

Polly's heart sank. She wasn't sure she could take much more of this date — not if she hoped to make it home alive!

⚜ Chapter 8 ⚜

*T*his is the pet store you go to?" Denise sniffed as they entered Salamander Sam's a few minutes later. She planted her hands on her hips and looked around. "*We* always go to Kit and Ka-poodle. They only carry top-of-the line pet products there."

Polly was too tired to even roll her eyes. She had to admit Denise had a point, though. Salamander Sam's was a little run-down. The floor looked like it hadn't been mopped, and several of the cages were empty. A bored-looking man with a long ponytail sat near the cash register, flipping through a magazine.

Polly didn't understand why they were there. The Kreeps had plenty of critters in their mansion: mice in the basement, bats in the eaves, and salamanders in the second-floor bathroom. In fact, now that Polly thought about it, their house was practically a zoo! *What could Vincent possibly want in a plain old pet shop?* she wondered.

Denise was peering into a cage of lop-eared rabbits. "Look at the cute bunnies," she squealed. "Vincent, come see!"

There was no answer. The girls looked around and saw Vincent disappear behind a green curtain at the back of the store.

Denise raised her eyebrows at Polly. Polly shrugged to say she didn't know what was back there. Denise straightened up and headed for the back of the store, with Polly close behind.

Behind the curtain, the room was darker. The air was moist and it seemed to press in close.

"It's like a jungle back here," Polly murmured. She brushed aside a hanging plant and squinted in the dim light. Along the walls, fish flitted back and forth in illuminated tanks. There were other tanks, too, filled with rocks or plants instead of water. Unlike the front of the store, this room was crowded. Even the air felt alive.

Vincent was hunched over a large glass cage, peering at something inside.

At first, Polly thought the cage was empty. All she could see were a few sticks and a big rock in the corner. Then she realized that what she'd mistaken for a rock was alive.

"It's a snake!" Polly said with a gasp.

"A python," Vincent corrected. "Isn't she beautiful?"

Denise shuddered. "I hate snakes."

"It's really big," Polly noted.

Vincent nodded. "Eighteen feet long. I wanted to buy her, but Mother was afraid she'd eat Esme."

"This snake could eat a person?" Denise asked worriedly.

"Oh, yes! Look." Vincent pointed into the cage. The snake's black tongue flicked in and out. "It's testing the air. It can smell us."

Denise gripped Polly's arm. "I think I need to leave," she whispered. "I'm scared of snakes."

"You can't leave yet," Vincent told her.

"You don't want me to leave?" For a second, Denise seemed to forget about the snake. She smiled happily at Vincent.

"No, you'll miss the best part," Vincent said. "It's almost feeding time."

Denise's smiled faded. "Feeding time," she murmured. She looked like she might faint.

At that moment, something caught the snake's attention. It began to uncoil. Denise let out a shriek and scrambled backward.

But she forgot that she was wearing skates. Her feet shot out from underneath her. Denise flapped her arms, trying to keep her balance. She grabbed on to the first thing she touched, which happened to be a cage of mice.

CRASH! Denise and the cage hit the floor. The door popped open, and the mice scurried out.

"Oh, no! Catch them!" Polly cried.

"Help! Get it away from me!" Denise shrieked as a mouse scuttled over her leg.

Polly tried to grab it, but the mouse

slipped between her fingers. "They're too quick!" she said. "We'll never be able to catch them all."

Vincent grinned. "We could let the snake out of the cage. It would catch those mice quick enough."

That was all Denise needed to hear. With a horrified screech, she scrambled to her feet and fled from the store, skating faster than Polly had ever seen her go.

On the way out, she almost ran over the shopkeeper. "What's going on back here?" the man asked, appearing in the doorway. When he saw Polly, Vincent, and the open mouse cage, he bellowed, "You kids get out of my store!"

Seconds later, Polly and Vincent found themselves out on the sidewalk. The storekeeper slammed the door behind them. "And don't come back!" he called through the glass.

Polly looked down the street. There was no sign of Denise. "She's probably halfway home by now," Polly said.

"Sorry about your friend," Vincent said to Polly.

"She's not really my friend," Polly told him.

"She's not?" Vincent looked surprised. He shrugged and added, "It's just as well. She wasn't very cool."

It was Polly's turn to be surprised. "You mean, you don't like Denise? Then why did you keep asking her to do stuff?"

"I was just being nice to her because I thought she was your friend."

"Are you sure you don't want Denise to be your girlfriend?" Polly asked.

Vincent's eyebrows shot up. "Girlfriend? What gave you *that* idea?"

"Nothing," Polly muttered. She didn't want to explain about Denise's crush, and how Polly had been trying to keep her from finding out the truth about the Kreeps.

Vincent looked at Polly and shook his head. "Polly, you have a pretty crazy imagination."

Polly couldn't believe it. Now even the Kreeps were telling her she was imagining things!

"But that's okay," Vincent added. "I like people with good imaginations. Come on. I'll race you home."

"No way," Polly said. "You'll beat me by a mile."

"No tricks. I promise. My wheels won't leave the ground," he added with a wink.

Polly stared at him. Did that mean what she thought it meant? Was Vincent actually telling her that he *could* fly?

She didn't have time to think about it, because a second later Vincent had zipped

89

away. "Last one there is a witch's wart!" he called back over his shoulder.

Polly leaped onto her bike. "I hope you're hungry, Vincent!" she yelled. "'Cause you're about to eat my dust!"

❄ Chapter 9 ❄

Monday morning, Polly got to school early. Long before the bell rang, she was waiting by the school doors. She wanted to catch Denise before classes started.

Polly figured Denise might be embarrassed about how silly she'd acted that weekend. She might even be mad. And if Denise was mad, who knew what she'd say about Polly and her family?

Polly didn't care anymore if Denise thought she was weird. *She* thought *Denise* was just plain rude — and rude was even worse than weird, in Polly's opinion. But she didn't want Denise to reveal the

Kreeps' secret. That might cause trouble for Polly's stepfamily. And Polly was just starting to enjoy having her stepfamily around.

Polly shifted her backpack from one shoulder to the other. Kids had started to arrive at school.

"Hey, Polly! Guess what?" Mike came bounding over to her. "We won the tournament this weekend!" he said.

"That's great, Mike," Polly said.

"So how did it go on Friday?" Mike asked. "I mean, with Denise coming to your house?"

Polly blew her bangs out of her eyes. "I'm not sure yet," she replied.

"Huh?" Mike's forehead wrinkled. "What do you mean?"

Polly didn't answer. A silver car had pulled up in front of the school, and Denise Dunleavy was climbing out. "Hold

92

on, Mike," Polly said, starting toward her. "I'll be right back."

When Denise saw Polly, her eyes narrowed into slits. *I was right*, Polly thought. *She's got it in for me.* Good thing she was there to talk to Denise early.

But as Polly walked toward Denise, Misty cut in front of her. She got to Denise first.

"Where were you all weekend?" Misty asked. "I called you a bunch of times. Didn't you get my messages?"

Denise was glaring at Polly and didn't answer. Misty followed her gaze and smirked. "So did you go over to Polly Winkler's *mansion* on Friday?" she sneered, loud enough for Polly to hear.

"Hey, Denise!" Polly called. She gave a big friendly wave and walked over to the two girls.

"What do *you* want?" Denise snapped.

"I have something for you," Polly said. When Denise didn't reply, she added, "It's from Vincent."

"Vincent?" Denise suddenly perked up.

Misty wrinkled her nose. "Who's Vincent?"

Polly could tell Denise wanted to know what Vincent had sent, but she didn't want to talk to Polly. Finally, Denise's curiosity won out. "Well, what is it?" she asked, impatiently.

"It's sort of personal," Polly said. She turned to Misty, "Sorry, I can't show you."

"Go on, Misty. Leave us alone," Denise said.

Misty folded her arms and huffed. But she did as Denise said.

Polly reached into her backpack. She pulled out Vincent's camera. "He was sorry you never got a chance to see this," she said, pressing a button.

A video of Denise appeared on the camera's tiny screen. It was the trip down from Lookout Point: Denise screaming and flapping her arms like a chicken . . . Denise running smack into a bush . . . Denise skating downhill rear end first.

"Isn't it great?" said Polly when the video clip was over. "I especially like the part where you swing around the tree branch."

"I look *awful*! You have to erase it!" Denise tried to snatch the camera out of Polly's hands.

Polly yanked it away. "Hold on. Not so fast. I haven't showed Mike yet."

"You'd better not show that to *anybody*, or you'll be sorry," Denise snarled through clenched teeth.

Polly shrugged. "All right. Whatever you say. But they're going to see it anyway."

"What do you mean?" asked Denise.

"Well, you know that TV show *Hilarious Home Videos*?" Polly replied. "Vincent wants to submit yours. You're going to be on national TV!"

"No!" Denise gasped. "He can't!"

"What's wrong?" Polly asked, pretending to be surprised. "I thought you wanted to be a star."

"You have to tell Vincent not to send that video," Denise said, grabbing Polly's arm. "Please, Polly? I'll be your friend forever."

Polly shook off Denise's hand. "Forget it, Denise," she snapped. "I wouldn't want you as a friend." She started to walk away. Then she paused and turned back. "But now that I think of it, there *is* something you can do."

"What is it?" asked Denise.

"Never say anything bad about my family again. *Ever*," Polly told her.

96

Denise's nostrils flared. Polly could tell she was thinking of a hundred mean things to say.

"All right," Denise agreed at last.

"Thanks, Denise. See you around." Polly turned and walked back to Mike just as the bell rang.

"What was *that* all about?" Mike asked as they went into the school.

Polly really wanted to show Mike the video. But she wasn't going to. If Denise could keep a secret, then so could Polly. "Nothing much," she told Mike. "Just catching up after the weekend."

Suddenly, there was a loud noise behind them. Polly and Mike turned in time to see the door to the boys' bathroom open. Damon emerged in a puff of purple smoke.

Now, Polly thought with a sigh, *if I can just keep my stepbrother from blowing up the school.*

97

Polly's adventures with
the Kreeps continue in

Meet the Kreeps
Kicking and Screaming

Turn the page for a sneak
peek . . . if you dare!

Polly looked up at the Puffins' goal. It was totally walled in, except for a small gap to the left. But the goalie was favoring the right side. Maybe she still had a chance. . . .

"Polly!" Mike yelled.

Polly glanced over and saw that he was wide open. She looked back toward the goal. All she could see could see was a cluster of yellow shirts. The gap in the Puffins' defense had started to close.

Polly desperately wanted to score the winning goal. But she knew she didn't have a clear shot. What's more, the Puffins' orange-haired midfielder had turned and was now charging toward her like an angry buffalo.

"Polly! I'm open!" Mike flailed his arms.

With a twinge of regret, Polly gave the ball a hard kick and sent it skidding across the grass to Mike.

The ball had only gone a few feet, though, when it gave a little jerk, as if it had come to the end of an invisible leash. Suddenly, it reversed direction and rolled back to Polly.

"Huh?" Polly blinked in surprise. But she didn't have time to wonder what happened. The orange-haired giant was almost on top of her. Polly could see bits of grass flying from the girl's churning cleats.

At the last second, Polly closed her eyes and booted the ball as hard as she could.

"Oof!" Polly grunted as the girl barreled into her. They both hit the ground, hard.

When Polly opened her eyes, she saw the ball sailing through the air. With a groan, she realized her shot had gone wide. She'd missed the goal by a mile.

Then, to her amazement, the ball began to curve.

Polly watched, openmouthed, as it drew a graceful half circle in the air and came down right in front of the Puffins' defense. It bounced between the legs of a fullback and continued on toward the goal.

The goalie knelt, ready to scoop it up. But once again, the ball seemed to change course. With a tiny swerve, it dodged the goalie's fingertips and rolled into the net.

The crowd exploded. As Polly picked herself up off the ground, her ears filled with the sound of cheering. *I did it!* she thought. She wasn't quite sure *how* she'd done it, but at the moment it didn't matter.

The orange-haired ogre stood up, too. She gave Polly a fierce look. "That wasn't possible!" she spat.

"Says you!" said Polly, with little smirk. Shaking her bangs out of her eyes, she turned and ran back to her teammates.

The Devils were beside themselves. They shouted and grinned and slapped Polly's back. They held out their hands to smack high five.

"Awesome, Polly!"

"That was incredible!"

"Way to go!"

"Devastating, darling! That was absolutely devastating!"

Polly turned and saw her stepmother standing between two of the soccer moms. Today Veronica was dressed like a gypsy fortune-teller, with a bloodred scarf tied over her hair and big, dangly hoop earrings. She was smiling and waving her black handkerchief like a flag. When she caught Polly's eye, she winked.

Suddenly, Polly felt uneasy.

She looked back at the goal, where the Puffins were still standing and shaking their heads. The orange-haired girl was right. The shot had been impossible. So how had Polly made it?

Could it have been more than just good luck and mad soccer skills?

Could it have been—magic?

Meet the Kreeps

Check out the whole spooky series!

#1: There Goes the Neighborhood

#2: The New Step-Mummy

#3: The Nanny Nightmare

#4: The Mad Scientist

#5: Three's a Krowd

Rotolo Middle School LMC